To my family and
bunnies everywhere

www.mascotbooks.com

For more information, please contact:
Mascot Books
560 Herndon Parkway
Herndon, VA 20170
info@mascotbooks.com

CPSIA Code: PRT0913A
ISBN: 1620863774
ISBN-13: 9781620863770

Library of Congress Control Number: 2013947748

Printed in the United States

BUTTONS THE BUNNY
of Button Cove Lane

Sue Murphy
Capobianco

BUTTONS' FAMILY PHOTO ALBUM

Freddy the cat, my Auntie Bubbles, cousins Elaine and Billy, and Uncle Eddie waving from Button Island

My father, me, and mother waving from Button Cove Lane

Buttons the Bunny of Button Cove Lane

Hopped into his kayak with his cousin Elaine.

The waters were choppy, the buoys were bobbing.

Buttons was rowing, his heart was a-throbbing.

"There's Button Island!" Elaine shouted out.

Uncle Eddie was waving while fishing about

For his favorite red cap that a gust of wind took,

With Freddy his cat, who was helping him look.

Elaine's brother, Billy, helped to bring in their boat

As Elaine and then Buttons tried to keep it afloat.

Auntie Bubbles called down to them all at the shore,

"There's carrots and cabbage, and clover and more

For you all to enjoy as a quick little snack

Up here at the house, on the table out back!"

They nibbled and munched and crunched through their lunch
As Elaine filled their cups full of strawberry punch.
"Listen to those wind chimes," Buttons said between bites.
"After lunch we'll find Billy and fly our new kites!"

But the wind was blowing harder, and the skies became black

So Buttons now decided that he'd better head back.

Buttons thanked Auntie Bubbles for the snacks and the treats

As she hugged him goodbye, she handed him sweets.

Elaine, her brother, Billy, and their little cat, Freddy,

Returned to the shore and helped Buttons get ready.

Uncle Eddie was still searching and waving goodbye
Despite catching seaweed, he still wanted to try.

As Buttons rowed quickly and he struggled and he fumbled,

He sang silly songs while the loud thunder rumbled.

And just when he thought his little boat would tip over

Around swam two harbor seals, Sandy and Dover!

They arrived just in time to guide Buttons back home

"Thank you, my friends, I felt so all alone!"

"You're welcome!" said the seals as they gave him a tow.

They could now see his house, every window aglow.

As Sandy and Dover gently pushed him ashore

Buttons gave them his sweets from Auntie Bubbles before.

Smiling, the seals swam through the rolling, stormy harbor

As Buttons ran up to meet his mother and his father.

As they hugged him and they dried him with some big fluffy towels

He began to warm up again despite the wind's howls.

He sat by the hearth in the overstuffed chair

With his favorite blue blanket and his brown teddy bear.

Mother placed his hot cocoa on the table nearby

With some cranberry cookies and asparagus pie.

As he sipped from his mug, Buttons let out a sigh.

He was glad to be home again, warm, cozy, and dry.

Safe from the thunder and lightning and rain

Was Buttons the Bunny of Button Cove Lane!

Until next time, little bun...

Happy dreams, everyone...

Sue Murphy Capobianco lives on the South Shore of Massachusetts with her husband, two children, and two cats. She draws inspiration for her stories from the wild bunnies that hop across her lawn and all around town. This is the first book in her *Button Tales* series. In the next adventure, Buttons welcomes a new arrival.

Have a book idea?
Contact us at:

Mascot Books
560 Herndon Parkway
Suite 120
Herndon, VA 20170

info@mascotbooks.com | www.mascotbooks.com